Summertime
&
The Livin' is Easy

By
Author/ Illustrator

EDWINA LOUISE DORCH

ISBN 978-1-956691-08-5 (softcover)
ISBN 978-1-956691-10-8 (hardcover)
ISBN 978-1-956691-09-2 (ebook)
Library of Congress Control Number: 2023901404

OrionPress
www.orionpressbooks.com
1382 Belmont Road, Raymond, WA 98577

Table of Contents

Dedication

To my grandson

Cassius Cannon

Born the Same Year

Barack Obama Became Our 44th President

To Caregivers

Middle-grade fiction is fiction intended for children aged between **8 and 11**. It's also called fiction for the in-between readers.

It serves as a bridge between simple children's stories and reading materials that are more emotionally or thematically advanced.

Epigraph

Excerpt From A Poem

Life Doesn't Frighten Me

By

Maya Angelou

Shadows on the wall

Noises down the hall

Life doesn't frighten me at all

Preface

Excerpt from the Song

Summertime when the livin' is easy

Fish are jumpin and the cotton is high

Your daddy's rich and your ma is good lookin'

So, hush little baby, don't you cry.

"Summertime" is a song composed in 1934

by George Gershwin

List of Characters

Jasmine, 10 years old

Frankie, 11 years old

Mama, Black-American

Stepdaddy, Black-American

Benji, Dog

Mr.s Harris, Suburban Caucasian-American Housewife

Dr. Harris, Suburban Caucasian-American Doctor

Cindy Harris, Suburban Caucasian American Tween

Angelina, A Hispanic Suburban House Maid

An African American City Bus Driver

Jasmine eyed the coins--dimes, nickels, quarters, and half-dollars--that covered the top of Mr. Harris' bedroom chest of drawers.

"How much money did all these coins add up to?" she wondered as she laid Mr. Harris' freshly washed laundry on his king-size bed. Overwhelmed with curiosity, she began to slide the coins into piles so it would be easier to count them. No, counting them would have to wait, because Mama had asked her to put Mr. Harris' just-washed laundry in his chest of drawers.

She opened his top drawer and a half-dozen tiny bottles rolled noisily forward. Surprised, she lifted one of them.

"Jack Daniels," she whispered.

Mama bounded up the stairs from the washroom in the basement and Jasmine quickly began to lay Mr. Harris' T-shirts in three rows side by side on top of the tiny bottles and closed his drawer.

Mama entered the Harris' bedroom, proceeded to their walk-in closet on the other side of the King-size bed and began to hang Mrs. Harris' sweaters on the top rung. When she finished hanging her sweaters, she picked up a pair of Mrs. Harris' shoes and put them in one of the cubbies on a wooden shoe rack spread across the back wall.

Jasmine entered the closet and noticed that many of Mrs. Harris' outfits still had a price tag on them. Mama put her hand in the small of Jasmine's back and nudged her out of the Harris' closet. A night stand stood beside Mrs. Harris' closet and a dozen white pill bottles of different sizes covered it. Jasmine lifted one and read the label.

"*Paxil,*" she pronounced the word slowly. Gently, Mama took the bottle from her hand and placed it back on the night table.

"Go put these sweaters in Cindy's closet," she said placing Cindy's sweaters in her arms and giving her a little push forward.

Jasmine walked down the hall to Cindy's room, walked to the other side of her canopied bed, and into her closet. Cindy's plastic rain boots sat near the entrance of the closet where her pink satin ballet shoes and her shiny tap dance shoes also sat. A dozen tennis shoes, of various colors, sat against the back wall of Cindy's closet. Jasmine hung Cindy's pastel sweaters neatly in her closet and walked across the room to a wall of books.

"Cindy has as many books as a bookmobile has," she thought and she stepped back to admire them, noticing the bright blue words 'Dyslexia Quest' flashing again and again on Cindy's computer screen.

"A game?" Jasmine wondered.

Jasmine was about to press the ENTER key when she heard Mrs. Harris and Cindy enter the front door downstairs. They had been back-to-school shopping at the neighborhood mall. Mrs. Haris, a woman who looked like a Barbie Doll, with snow white hair, green eyes, and pink lips set an assortment of shopping bags of various sizes and colors on the living room floor.

Cindy ran over to Jasmine and the two girls started hand clapping, slowly at first, then faster and faster, and with more intricate clap patterns. The goal of the hand clap game was to anticipate when a partner was about to change a pattern and to never miss a clap. Mrs. Harris' marveled at the speed of their complex hand clap patterns.

"Is everything ready for the party tonight, Peaches? Mrs. Harris asked.

"Yes, Mrs. Harris. The prime rib is in the oven, the candied yams and crescent rolls are covered on the stovetop and the key lime pie is in the refrigerator. All you need to do is serve it," Mama smiled.

"Daddy," Cindy exclaimed as Dr. Harris entered the front door. He put his medical bag in the hall closet, and Cindy ran and jumped into his arms, wrapping her arms around his neck, and her legs around his waist.

"Hey, Baby Doll," Dr. Harris responded affectionately.

"Your daughter ordered a shrimp cocktail for lunch today, but didn't eat a bite, then asked me to buy her gumdrops from the candy store. Ate most of them and spilled the rest all over the rug in the car before we got home," Mrs. Harris lamented.

"Candy is the reason I'm so sweet. Right, Daddy?" Cindy quizzed her father.

"Right," her father agreed and he continued to smile lovingly at her.

"Excuse me, Dr. Harris, would you mind checking in Jasmine's ear again? See if she's recovered from that ear infection she had," Mama asked.

"Not at all, Peaches." He put Cindy down, walked to the hall closet, took his otoscope out of his medical bag, strolled over to Jasmine, bent slightly from the waist, looked directly into her eyes, and smiled.

His eyes looked like her brother's sapphire cat-eye marbles. Jasmine tilted her head to one side. He put his otoscope in her ear and repositioned it twice before he stood up again.

"Looks good, Jazzy. Your ear will be fine," he said before he lowered his long, thick, black eyelashes and looked at her bare legs and tattered shoes held on by safety pins rather than buckles.

Mrs. Harris noticed Mr. Harris looking at the safety pins that held Jasmine's shoes on her feet.

"Oh, Peaches, I almost forgot, I've got some shoes and clothes that Cindy has never worn that might fit Jasmine. They're in her bedroom. I'll get them for you. Be right back." She took off her pink high heels and ran up the stairs.

"Are you going to take the nurse's exam next month, Peaches?" Mr. Harris asked.

"Yes. I've been studying with Angie, your neighbor, Mrs. Jones' maid down the street," she replied.

Mr. Harris nodded, took a few steps, and looked up the stairs to see if his wife was coming. He didn't see her.

"So, is Isaac going to be able to clean windows during the winter months?" he asked.

"God willing," Mama replied. She took a few steps and she too glanced up the stairs to see if Mrs. Harris was coming.

"Food smells wonderful… as usual. My interns need a home-cooked meal. They'll think my wife cooked for them. And she won't tell them any different," he said.

"Well, I made your favorite… key lime pie," she smiled hearing something thumping down the stairs as Mrs. Harris descended pulling a rolling duffle bag behind her.

"I was going to box these and give them to Goodwill but might as well give them to Jasmine. Hope they fit her," she said.

"Very kind of you, Mrs. Harris," Mama smiled, rolled the bag to the front closet, took off her apron, opened the front door and she and Jasmine stepped out.

"Bye," Cindy waved dramatically.

"Bye," Jasmine and Mama returned her wave.

✻✻

Magnolia trees with sprawling limbs shaded the sidewalk as Mama and Jasmine walked briskly down the street inhaling the fragrance of their thick cream-colored blossoms. The only noise was that of the lawnmowers and the electric trimmers that Hispanic yard men used to trim the bordering boxwood bushes. A few blocks down they met Angelina, the Jones' house maid.

"Tienes hermosas trenzas hoy," Angie said to Jasmine, admiring her braided hair.

"Eres demasiado amable Angie. Mi madre lo hizo," Jasmine replied indicating her mother had braided it.

As they neared a massive wrought iron gate, a guard sitting in a guard house at the entrance to the neighborhood electronically opened the gate. Silently, the massive twenty-foot-high gate doors swung open from the middle. Mama, Angelina and Jasmine left the gated neighborhood, walked down the concrete sidewalk, and headed for the bus stop.

"Peaches, you should tell Isaac to apply for a city job because city jobs offer low-cost health insurance plans," Angelina suggested.

"Thanks, Angie, but a city job requires a high school degree and Isaac doesn't have one. He quit high school to work the family farm and to support his widowed mother. So, he can't apply right now. But when he finishes taking evening GED classes and passes the GED exam, he'll apply," Mama assured her.

"I understand. My husband does not speak English well. So, he must pass the city English exam before he can apply. But, when he passes that exam and gets a city job, we can get health insurance, then we can buy the insulin I need to treat my diabetes. I can't afford to buy insulin right now. But if I don't start taking insulin soon, I will lose my feet like my mother did a few years ago," she revealed to Mama.

"Oh, no," Mama gasped.

Garbage trucks, furniture trucks, and Amazon trucks rambled busily down the highway as they walked three blocks to a glass-covered bus stop and Angelina took a radio out of a duffle bag and turned it on.

"Bésame, Bésame mucho," A singer sung a love song in Spanish.

"Kiss Me, Kiss Me a lot," Jasmine translated the words of the love song.

They waited twenty minutes before the front fender of the air-conditioned city bus swerved close to the curb. The bus driver electronically unlocked the side luggage compartment and stepped out.

He did not have earphones in his ears, but still, he had a happy jingle in his step, as he slung their belongings into the storage compartment. His coarse hair was cut close to his head. His khaki uniform was heavily starched and his black shoes glistened with shoe polish.

Their baggage stored, Mama, Angie, and a half-a-dozen other maids boarded and began chatting about their chores that day and the nature of the people whose houses they cleaned.

Jasmine was the last to board and she sat down in the front seat, across from the bus driver, who electronically closed the hull and then the passenger doors.

"Got something for ya," he grinned, opened his glove compartment, took out an Orange Tootsie Roll lollipop, and handed it to her.

"Your favorite, right?" he smiled. His brown eyes twinkled.

"Right," she agreed.

"So, what do you want to be when you grow up Jazzy?" he asked as he effortlessly maneuvered the city bus in and out of the busy highway traffic.

"A preacher" she grinned proudly.

"Is your father a preacher?" he asked as they whizzed by car dealerships, discount clothing outlets, and electrical plants.

No, he died at war a few years ago," she looked away.

"I'm so sorry to hear that," he consoled her.

"What you gonna preach about?" he tried to change the subject.

"The Beatitudes," she perked up.

"Look at you" he grinned, electronically opening the back door and the luggage compartment for Angelina and the other maids to deboard, and collect their belongings. Mama walked to the front of the bus.

"Jasmine did you thank the bus driver for that lollipop?" she asked.

"Like makin kids happy. So, givin them Lollipops is not a problem for me. What's your name?" he asked Mama.

"Peaches" she replied.

"Because of her skin color," Jasmine offered.

"Um hum, I see what you're saying Jazzy. She does have a beautiful skin color" he nodded.

Mama and Jasmine deboarded at the next bus stop, retrieved the duffle bag from the luggage compartment and headed for their neighborhood grocery store. A man with mangled hair and no shoes lay in front of the grocery store doorway. Mama and Jasmine stepped cautiously over him and entered the store.

Inside, a man with taunt, leathery, olive skin and thick salt-and-pepper curls mopped the linoleum floor with Pinesol. Mama stepped around him and walked down the next aisle. Jasmine scurried to the counter where she ogled rolls and rolls of Orange, Root Beer, Cherry, Lime, and Butterscotch Life Savers candy.

"Here you go Jazzy," the store owner handed her a piece of bubble gum he kept behind the counter for neighborhood children.

Jasmine thanked him and waited at the door for Mama. Mama paid the grocer, put her groceries into the same duffle bag that Mrs. Harris had given her, and leaving the store, handed a pint of milk to the man lying on the ground, now whispering to himself.

"Gracias," the man grinned a toothless grin, eyeing the fine wisp of brown hair around her heart-shaped face.

"He's homeless, Jazzy," she said putting her hand in the small of Jasmine's back and guiding her to the stoplight. They crossed the bridge, walked down the sidewalk and headed for home.

***

Mama and Jasmine arrived home just as Stepdaddy and Frankie were unloading their window cleaning equipment from the back of the family pickup truck.

"Careless," Stepdaddy growled at Frankie. Mama's eyebrows furrowed and she looked from Stepdaddy to Frankie, then back at Stepdaddy.

"He left one of my wash buckets behind and when I went back to get it, it was gone and I ain't got no money to replace it," he snarled, storing a large bottle of vinegar he used to wash windows in the garage.

"He was of no help at all. He followed behind the electricians, trying to learn their business the whole day. Asked a thousand questions. Irritated them and succeeded in cleaning only a few windows. Worthless," he complained. Looking at Frankie, whose nose was running because he had been crying, Mama assessed the situation.

"Children make mistakes," Mama declared before going to the refrigerator for an egg, to the cupboard for cornmeal, and to the faucet for a cup of water. She stirred all the ingredients in a bowl, made corn bread, put it in the oven, and then heated a pot of the neckbones and pinto beans that she had cooked the day before.

Jasmine placed water glasses, bowls, and spoons around the table for each family member and they all sat down to eat. Mama began to say grace but before she could finish, Stepdaddy began eating his corn bread. He looked at each person at the table, snorted, corn bread crumbs sticking to the corners of his mouth.

"Eat that fat," he scowled at Frankie. "Might be all you have to eat one day. Po' folks don't turn their nose up at fat. Gotta learn how to stomach it," he scolded. Frankie looked at Mama. Her brow furrowed for the second time that evening, but she said nothing.

"You gonna sit there till you eat it, so you might as well eat it now," he barked.

Mama stood up from the table.

"Jazzy, I have been on my feet all day and I'm more tired than usual. Would you wash the dishes for me tonight?" she asked.

"Yes, ma'am," Jasmine exhaled deeply. She too was tired but didn't say so. Mama walked down the hall and disappeared into the laundry room. Stepdaddy continued to stare at Frankie. And, withering under Stepdaddy's continuous gaze, Frankie put the fat in his mouth and

tried to swallow it. He gagged violently and spit brown
bile into his hand.

"Don't matter. You gonna sit there until you eat it
all," he roared, then stood up. His huge belly hung over
his belt and he belched loudly before he grabbed his chair,
meandered down the dimly lit hallway, out the screen door,
and on to the front porch. Hearing the screen door slam,
Mama came out of the laundry room, looked at Frankie's
plate, picked up the fat, and threw it into the garbage can
near the back door.

"Come outside and cool off. It's hot in here," she
coaxed. Frankie slowly stood up. Mama put her arms

around him and the two walked down the narrow hallway, out of the screen door, and onto the front porch.

"Jasmine, bring me a glass of water and put ice in it," Stepdaddy yelled from the front porch.

"Yes, sir," she answered as she walked to the refrigerator door, opened it, and took out an ice tray. And, ice tray in hand, she walked to the sink, ran tap water over the tray, filled a water glass with ice, and headed for the screen door.

Outside, Stepdaddy sat in a kitchen chair with his feet up on the banister. Jasmine handed the water glass to him. But distracted by the chirp of a cricket she thought she heard behind him, she spilled some of the water into his lap. Annoyed by her carelessness, he angrily swatted the back of her legs and she fell to her knees.

"Watch what you're doing, girl!" he growled.

"Yes, sir," she cowered, glancing sideways at Mama. But she looked away.

Jasmine's lip quivered as she returned to the kitchen and began washing first the glasses, then the bowls, then the bean pot. Her shoulders sagged and she sighed as she scrubbed the cornbread pan with the scouring pad.

She moaned, sniffled, and gulped before she suddenly stopped, and abruptly jerked a Holy Cross necklace hanging around her neck. Breaking its clasp, she fiercely flung it across the room.

"I'm not going to believe in you anymore, God, cuz you don't treat everybody the same. You're kind to some folks but not to me," she sobbed.

Relieved by such a deviant act, she wiped her face with the back of her arms, turned off the kitchen lights, walked down the dingy hallway, out of the screen door, and onto the front porch.

Stepdaddy sat in his kitchen chair on one side of the porch and Mama, Frankie, and their Collie, Benji sat on the concrete porch on one side. Jasmine walked over and sat next to them on the concrete porch. The crickets were louder than usual.

"Why is it that you can hear crickets, but you can't see 'em?" Jasmine asked the group.

"I don't know, but I saw the one that got you into trouble just now," Frankie said.

"What did he look like," she questioned.

"Looked like a troublemaker," he grinned. "Nah, he looked like a grasshopper," he giggled.

"Mama, do crickets look like grasshoppers?" Jasmine asked.

"Kinda. Both sing a song, but grasshoppers are a little bigger," Mama replied.

"The same but a little bigger. Why?" she wondered.

"I was right" Frankie declared. "I'm always right," he pushed against her shoulder with his. She swayed and fell over into Mama. Stepdaddy noticed.

"Well, Mr. Bigshot, you were wrong today when you left my bucket behind," he stood up and slid his calloused feet across the porch to where Frankie sat.

Stepdaddy lifted Frankie from the group. One of his arms circled Frankie's neck and his other arm circled

Frankie's knees. Frankie writhed, twisted, and gasped for air. Benji stood up, his ears raised and he began to growl.

"Let him go," Mama demanded. Jasmine's eyes widened. She had never heard her mother speak sharply to anyone before and she sat stunned.

Immediately, Stepdaddy released Frankie, eyes batting rapidly in disbelief at the tone of Mama's voice, a tone he had never heard before. Upset, Mama headed for the screen door but turned for a moment.

"Jasmine I need to prepare and serve the meal at the Harris' swim party tomorrow because I need money to buy you and Frankie's back-to-school supplies. That means I won't be home until suppertime. So, you and Frankie have cereal and milk for breakfast and bologna sandwiches for lunch," she said before disappearing into the house.

Seeing Mama's courage, Jasmine scurried over to Frankie, hugged him, and rocked him back and forth. Stepdaddy gulped water from the glass Jasmine had given him earlier, belched loudly and slid his feet with crooked, knotted and gnarled toes across the concrete porch and entered the screen door.

"Bear" Frankie sneered and the two dared to snicker, momentarily, safe from the beast.

"Let's play hide-and-seek," Frankie proposed.

"Okay. But you be 'the seeker' first," Jasmine suggested.

"I'm always 'the seeker'," Frankie moaned.

"That's not true. I was 'the seeker' last time, remember?" she queried.

"Okay, but don't go so far away this time," he insisted.

"Promise," she agreed. Frankie hid his head in his arm on a near by tree and began counting backward. "Ten… nine… eight."

Jasmine ran away and crouched in their neighbor's basement window, her knees to her chest. A chartreuse firefly glided lazily by her and she marveled at it.

"Why was it most fireflies had yellow tails but, every summer, a few had green tails?" she wondered.

"Seven… six… five," Frankie continued counting. Benji came up to her and she shooed him away, her eyes searching the warm, humid air for mosquitoes.

Frankie finished counting, walked to the back yard and started searching inside their garage. She prepared to run but he saw her and both ran towards the tree-base, tagging it at the same time before collapsing on the curb grass.

A Thunderbird glided stylishly as if the warm summer breeze carried it. Frankie licked the tip of his right thumb to claim it.

"Tagged it before you did" he claimed. She did not argue. Instead, she looked at an area between her and her neighbor's house where she had previously been hiding.

"While I was hidin, I saw a firefly, color of lime soda,"she said.

"Did not," he disputed her claim.

"Did too. Over there, where I was hidin," she insisted.

"Let's go find him," Frankie said.

Just then, Stepdaddy appeared on the front porch. Frankie's pupils dilated and Jasmine gulped. Neither moved.

"Jasmine, c'mere," he commanded.

Their eyes widened and for a moment she remained where she was. They looked at one another. Then she stood, walked cautiously toward him, and stopped a few feet away.

'Yes sir" she whispered, looking at the ground rather than looking directly at him.

"There's no bread in the breadbox to make sandwiches for our lunches tomorrow. Go to the store and get some bread," he commanded rambling a few feet forward toward her, and dramatically pressing some money into the palm of her hand.

"Yes sir," she muttered. She was aware that she was cowering but not brave enough to do otherwise.

"Get down there and get back. Take Frankie with you. And don't be fooling around like you usually do," he scowled, ignoring her cowering demeanor.

"Yes, sir," she whispered, her eyes lowered.

Frankie, who had been lying still on the curb grass, afraid to move and draw attention to himself, now stood grabbed Benji's collar, walked him to the back of the house and locked him behind the backyard fence.

"Stay," he said to Benji, then he walked to Jasmine's side, they grinned a sigh of relief, and headed to the grocery store to get a loaf of bread for bologna sandwiches, for lunch, the next day.

✱✱✱✱

A block down from their house, an El Camino drove by, and Jasmine tagged it before he did. Another block down, Frankie discovered a silver bicycle rim lying in the middle of the sidewalk. He stood it up, and began to roll it down the sidewalk.

"So, why do you think some fireflies' tails are green when most of the others are yellow?" she asked.

"Biology" he responded authoritatively.

"Explain?" she said.

"Heredity," he responded.

"Meaning," she said.

"Genes," he replied

"Genes," she repeated.

"Can't see 'em. But they control stuff," he said.

"Like God," she said.

"Like God," he shook his head.

The moon lit up a sinister-looking house with shingles missing from its roof and its windows boarded.

"I heard that house got ghosts," Frankie declared.

"Don't either," she said.

"Umm-hmm," he persisted.

She stopped, crossed her arms, raised her chin defiantly in the air and stomped her foot. "Don't believe in nothing I can't see," she blurted out.

"You believe in God and you can't see him," he countered.

"Nope. Not anymore," she asserted.

"Ooh, Jasmine! God gonna strike you dead," he warned.

"Won't. Can't. Cuz he don't exist!" she maintained.

"Bet you won't go inside that house," he said raising his hand and crossing his fingers, daring her to go.

She stared at the door, looked at him, thought for a moment, raised her hand, and crossed her fingers accepting his dare. He grinned mischievously.

Her eyes widened and she dashed wildly towards the house. She stumbled on the stairs, stood up, started to turn back, but with a burst of courage, grabbed the doorknob, and twisted it.

It was completely dark inside. A wind whistled through the rooms and whirled around her legs. She shivered, gulped, turned, and darted back to the sidewalk where Frankie stood bent over in laughter.

"Why'd you run back?" he questioned her.

"Cuz," she snapped.

"Afraid of ghosts, that's why," he blurted.

"Am not. Stepdaddy said not to fool around and we need to get to the store and get back," she explained.

The two crossed a concrete bridge over some railroad tracks and stopped to look down.

They could barely see glimmers of the silver railroad tracks below. Impulsively, she grabbed the wheel from him and lifted it high in the air.

"Don't! I want it!" he cried.

"Can't take it into the store with you" she scolded. She held the wheel high above her head, pulled her arm back as far as she could, and with all her might, heaved it down, and onto the railroad tracks.

He stamped his foot and narrowed his eyes, and his lip turned downward. But she ignored his pout, rolled her eyes, clicked her tongue, and walked on while he lagged behind her, brooding and kicking anything in front of him.

Approaching the parking lot of the grocery store, she saw the same homeless man that she and Mama had seen earlier. Frankie approached. The green neon lights on the grocery door flashed the words RALPH'S LIQUORS.

She placed both her hands flat against the door and an electric current shot through her body. Her pupils dilated. She felt hot and then cold and her stomach heaved as if she was going to vomit. She turned around and faced Frankie.

"Where's the money?" she exclaimed.

"You don't have it," he shrieked.

"No, … "I musta thrown it over with the wheel," she exclaimed. They ran to the bridge and looked over.

They batted and squinted their eyes but there was no sign of the wheel or the money. A white Cadillac rolled royally by. But, neither noticed.

"Help me, God," she whispered. A raven flapped its wings overhead and a mouse scurried around them heading towards a gap between the bridge and the brush. She squealed and jumped aside to let it pass but Frankie ran after it. It ran faster and disappeared into the brush.

He turned and looked at her. A tear rolled slowly down her cheek, into the corner of her mouth and she began to tremble. He put his arm around her shoulders.

"Don't cry, Jazzy," he tried to calm her. "I'll go down and find it for you," he offered.

"No, you don't have a flashlight and Auntie said not to go down there cuz snakes with light bulb heads are down there, and they lead children off into the brush, and they're never seen again," she warned.

"That can't be true!" his eyebrows furrowed; his mouth swayed to the side.

He looked at the gap between the bridge and the brush where the mouse had gone. He squeezed through it and held out his hand. She looked up at the sky for guidance. There was none. She inhaled and squeezed through.

*****

The two children had not taken more than a few steps when they began to slide uncontrollably down the steep slant of the hill. Their arms flailing about, they tried to grab branches of the brush, but when they did so, the branch thistles pierced their hands, and bleeding, they let go of them and stumbled chaotically over their own feet and each other.

"Frankie!" she screamed. Ahead of her, he turned but didn't see her.

"Jazzy where are you?" he yelled.

"Here!" she shrieked feeling the pinch of an open safety pin on her shoe strap.

"I've fallen into a manhole. Help me!" she gulped.

His eyes darted back and forth as he pushed the brush aside and climbed back up the hill. Over and over, he stumbled and slid downward until a large thorn caught his shirt and held him in place.

"Jazzy where are you," he called out to her.

"Here," she screamed. He took a few steps forward and leaned over. All he could see was her head and her two arms. Not knowing what to do, he grabbed the neck of her blouse while she used her foot to push herself out of the hole.

"I almost lost my shoe," she whispered once out, rubbing her wet nose with the back of her arm. He put his arm around her shoulder and he let her rest for a moment.

"There are snakes in these bushes. Let's go," he said, offering his hand to pull her to her feet and this time they turned their feet sideways to slow their descent.

Once on the ground, they batted their eyes adjusting them to the dim light. They looked up to the bridge and the moon beyond that. The railroad tracks stretched out before them for as far as they could see and they began to walk and search for the wheel and the bread money.

They examined the ground and jumped from one tie to the next thirty-nine times before she stopped.

"It's no use. I give up," she said, "We'll never find that money in the dark."

"Then what we gonna do?" he asked.

She felt tired and sat down on one of the wooden ties, pulled her knees to her chest, and laid her head on her knees. Hundreds of gnats surrounded her head and the no-see-ums bit her arms and legs. She looked up. One star in the sky was far brighter than the other.

"Probably Jupiter or Venus, not a star," she thought.

"Why are some stars brighter than others?" she asked aloud.

"Cause some are closer to us than others," he replied just as a bright, round, light blasted out of the darkness. The light flooded the area blinding them.A train whistle blew loudly, three times and the shiny steel frame of a train appeared.

"Frankie?" she yelled his name and squinted in the dark. There was silence. She rubbed and batted her eyes and yelled his name again.

Out of the dark, he ran up to her grinning mischievously. "Thought it killed me, didn't you?" he blurted.

"You're crazy!" she shoved him.

"Like a fox," he started dancing around her. She chased him for a minute and then stopped abruptly.

"Let's go home," she said and they began a slow and cautious ascent back up the hill to the bridge.

Crossing the bridge, they walked a block down the sidewalk passing the haunted house.

"O-o-h, you opened that door and now it's closed again," he said astonished.

"Don't try to pretend a ghost closed that door while we were on the tracks. Cause I told you I don't believe in nothing I can't see," she said.

"Believe in Santa Claus and never seen him," he challenged.

"Don't believe in him no more either!" she answered.

"That means you don't believe in Christmas. So, you a sinner, ah pagan. Yeah, yeah, you ah pagan, is what you is," he reasoned.

"I'm not a sinner. Not a pagan either!" she said swiveling her neck and clicking her tongue emphatically.

"You don't believe in god cause you can't see him but you believe in crickets and you never see them. So, you

ah,ah,…ah 'infidel.' Yeah, that's what Pastor would say…
you ah 'infidel'. He calls folks that when he's all fired up
about something," he grinned.

"I believe in crickets cuz they make a sound and no-
see-ums cuz they bite" she argued. Under the moonlight,
a glistening Ford convertible rolled by and its driver made
its engine growl. Their eyes widened and enthusiastically,
they both licked the tip of their thumbs to claim it.

So, whatcha gonna tell him?" he asked.

"Truth," she replied emphatically.

"That you threw the wheel over the bridge and onto
the railroad tracks. You crazy?" he blurted.

"What else am I gonna say?" she asked.

"All I know is you gonna wish there was a God cuz
you gonna get a whoopin you won't forget," he declared.
They approached their house and sat on the front stoop.
It was humid and moisture was now forming on the grass.

******

Frankie walked to the back of the house and returned pulling a go-cart with a rope. Benji walked beside him, tongue dripping.

A long slab of wood nailed to the side of his square wooden seat served as the brakes for the go-cart and its wheels came from a wagon he'd found in the alley behind their house.

He used a piece of rope tied to the slab in the front to turn the cart to the right or the left. He also used the rope to pull it forward and he pulled it to the sidewalk in front of their house and began to hammer the slab of wood on side of it.

"My brakes 'bout to go out... got to go look for another, stronger slab of wood tomorrow. Gonna search that haunted house," he grinned at her. She shuttered at the thought of him going inside the haunted house.

"I'm gonna tape my radio to the side of my cart so I can listen to music while I ride" he looked over to see what she thought of his idea.

"Yeah, right," she said.

"Oh, ye of little faith. I'm gonna be an engineer one day. Gonna go to the moon and back. You'll see. Hop on," he commanded as he began to pull the go-cart down the sidewalk.

At the street corner. Frankie looked down a steep hill into the darkness and a mischievous grin skipped across his face. He looked at her and then down the hill.

"Ride downhill? In the dark? You must be crazy!" she exclaimed. But, ignoring the fear in her voice, he held up his hand and crossed his fingers, a signal he dared her to go downhill in the dark on the go-cart.

Her brow furrowed. Bits of trash blew in circles in the middle of the street carried by the summer breeze. She looked down the hill and shook her head from side to side, but then, held up her hand and crossed her fingers, accepting his dare.

He began to push the cart slowly at first with one foot,but after a few steps, he hopped into the cart seat just as the wheels started spinning. As the cart sped up, it began to sway noisily from side to side.

Their eyes were filled with delight at the speed that the cart was going.Their nostrils flared and their mouths opened to take in more oxygen. Benji's tail wagged and he barked as he romped alongside the speeding cart. Halfway down the hill, a hole in the middle of the street made the cart leap into the air and plop down nosily onto the concrete.All the boards creaked and the axles on the wheels squealed as if they needed to be oiled.

The momentum grew, and the wheels turn faster and faster, and near the bottom of the hill, an old jalopy junk truck suddenly entered the intersection in front of them.

Frankie yanked the slab of wood that served as his brake, but it splintered, and broke off in his hand when it slammed against the concrete. Still trying to avoid the jalopy, he jerked the rope on the right side of the go-cart. But the cart overturned throwing them onto the concrete street. The jalopy truck sped off into the darkness.

The two lay near the intersection with skinned knees and elbows. They looked at each other, then at the mangled go-cart. She giggled, stumbled to her feet and bushed herself off. Then she held out her hand and pulled him to his feet.

He stood in the middle of the street with his hands on hips, shaking his head, and wondering how long it would take him to reassemble his beloved cart. She lifted a slab of wood that had previously been the front end of the cart and he lifted the rest and they walked back to the top of the hill.

They laid parts of the mangled go-cart in the garage. Frankie kneeled and lamented his demolished cart. Jasmine let Benji drink from the water hose and then locked him inside the backyard fence.

Frankie felt a mosquito bite him and he swatted his neck. "No trouble deciding whether mosquitos exist or not," he grinned.

"Their welts prove it, don't they?" she responded. The firefly with the green tail floated lazily between them. They stood with their mouths open and watched it ascend, marveling at it before it floated silently out of their reach.

"We gonna git in trouble if we stay out here any longer," he sighed.

"Yeah, I know," she agreed and the two walked towards the screen door and slowly down the hall and stopped in front of their mother's bedroom door.

****

The two children stood outside their parents' bedroom and looked at each other as if this was the last time they would see each other, then Jasmine knocked on their door.

Her mother awoke. "Hum?" she asked.

"Stepdaddy gave me some money to go to the store and get some bread for our lunches tomorrow but I lost the money on the way," Jasmine whispered.

"I bought some bread at the store on the way home. I probably left it in the washroom when I was sorting the clothes Mrs. Harris gave us. So, go to bed," she said. She sounded groggy.

In disbelief, the two scurried to the laundry room. There they discovered a loaf of Wonder bread sitting on top of the washing machine. Mama had sorted the clothes Mrs. Harris had given her into piles of light and dark clothes and a shiny pair of black, patent leather shoes sat next to the two piles of clothes.

"Now THIS is a miracle," Frankie proclaimed with authority as Jasmine lifted the patent leather shoes and marveled at their shininess.

"New shoes to start the school year," she said to herself.

She unfastened the safety pins where the buckles should have been on her old shoes and tried on her shiny new shoes. They fit her feet, and without taking them off, she walked towards the kitchen and towards the bread box.

As she put the bread in the bread box, he noticed her necklace on the floor near the kitchen sink. He walked across the room, picked it up, and turned to examine her face, searching for an explanation for why her necklace was on the floor. She said nothing.

Lacking an answer for why the necklace was on the floor, he lifted it, walked back to where she stood, spun her around, fastened the chain at the back of her neck, and straightened it on her chest.

Just this past Sunday, in church, Pastor said, "*Faith is the substance of things hoped for, evidence of things not seen.* Hebrews 11:1. You gotta stop playing tic-tac-toe in church!" he scolded, wagging his finger at her. He looked at the bread box, shook his head, and disappeared down the dim hallway for bed.

A breeze gently blew the kitchen curtains, beckoning Jasmine towards them. Slowly she walked over to them and looked up at the sky. For several moments, her hazel eyes probed the sky searching for answers. None were provided.

"God must see people the way I see stars in the sky... hard to tell one from the other," she thought.

Afterword

Excerpt From a Poem

Being the Mother of a Black Child

By

Mona Lake Jones

Being the mother of a Black child ain't no easy thing

You go to call on Jesus and listen to the angels sing.

They said you were what? That word is out of style.

Next time they call you names just raise your head and smile.

Tell them that you're proud of the color of your skin.

What counts is not the outside wrapping

but the character within.

About the Author

Edwina L. Dorch is a psychologist who lives on a barrier island off the Florida Coast. She is also a contemporary, abstract, minimalist artist who paints female figures and seascapes. Her paintings appear in a number of Galleries of Local Artists along the Florida A1A highway.

A Treat for the Reader

A Few Works of Art by the Author

Surfer Girl #12

Snow White #1

Purchased Online: Etsy Shop

https://www.etsy.com/shop/DorchAbstractArt?ref=shop_
onboarding&ele=shop_open

A Suggestion for the Reader

For Valentine's Day

Give

An Adult Novella by the Author

Amazon Books

https://www.amazon.com/dp/1663234051/
ref=sr_1_1?crid=193DUKRMQTDUL&keywords=vanilla%2C+
cinnamon+and+dark+chocolate&qid=
1656527303&s=books&sprefix=%2Cstripbooks%2C83&sr=1-1

Author Contact Information

Goodreads

https://www.goodreads.com/author/show/19456345.Edwina_Louise_Dorch

Instagram

https://www.instagram.com/dorchartcolortherapy/

To Caregivers

What you are about to read is a _short_ story.

The Nature of Short Stories

What is a definition of short story?

A short story is fictional work of prose that is shorter in length than a novel. Edgar Allan Poe, in his essay "The Philosophy of Composition," said that a short story should be read in one sitting, anywhere from a half hour to two hours.

In contemporary fiction, a short story can range from 1,000 to 20,000 words.

Because of the shorter length, a short story usually focuses on one plot, one main character (with a few additional minor characters), and one central theme, whereas a novel can tackle multiple plots and themes, with a variety of prominent characters.

Some Famous Short Stories Are:

- Washington Irving, "Rip Van Winkle" (1819)
- Edgar Allan Poe, "The Tell-Tale Heart" (1843)
- Charles Dickens, A Christmas Carol (1843)
- Henry James, "The Turn of the Screw" (1898)
- Daphne du Maurier, "The Birds" (1952)
- Philip K. Dick, "The Minority Report" (1956)
- Toni Cade Bambara, "The Lesson"(1972)
- Jamaica Kincaid, "Girl" (1978)

For Public Librarians

Augusta Baker was a Harlem branch librarian during the 1930s and 1940s who helped promote books for and about young people of color.

She also led a storytelling training program and became the first African American to head a division of The New York Public Library—youth services.

Youth Book Club Questions

1. Compare Jasmine and Cindy's shoes.
2. Compare Stepdaddy to the bus driver.
3. Why is Jasmine attending to differences.
4. What do you think of Frankie's answers.

African American Children's Books

According to the University of Madison, Wisconsin researchers (2020), **more than half** of K-12 public school students in the US are Black, American Indian, Hispanic or Asian. Yet less than 15 percent of children's books over the past two decades have contained multicultural characters or story lines.

The African American Literature Book Club compiled a list of 100 books for African American children's books. All books are chosen to affirm African American children and their experiences.

A Reader's Call to Action

Submit an Amazon Book Review

Before you can post a review, you must meet the eligibility requirements given in the Community Guidelines. Your submission must follow our Community Guidelines or we won't post the review.

1. Go to the product detail page for the item. If you've placed an order for the item, you can also go to Your Orders

2. Click Write a customer review in the Customer Reviews section.

3. Select a Star Rating.

4. A green check mark shows for successfully submitted ratings.

5. (Optional) Add text, photos, or videos and click Submit.

Submit a Goodreads Book Review

1. Navigate to the page of the book you'd like to review (you can find it by searching for it in the search bar in the header).
2. Underneath the book's cover image, hover over the stars until the desired number of stars is highlighted, then click on them to rate the book.
3. A pop-up menu will appear above the stars. Click on the Write a review text.
4. Enter your review on the following page and click on Save to submit.

And, Finally, To Help You to Remember

Reader Notes